THE
ROOTIN' TOOTIN'
BUGLE BOY

OTHER YOUNG YEARLING BOOKS
BY PATRICIA REILLY GIFF YOU WILL ENJOY:

YEARLING BOOKS/YOUNG YEARLINGS/YEARLING CLASSICS are designed especially to entertain and enlighten young people. Patricia Reilly Giff, consultant to this series, received her bachelor's degree from Marymount College and a master's degree in history from St. John's University. She holds a Professional Diploma in Reading and a Doctorate of Humane Letters from Hofstra University. She was a teacher and reading consultant for many years, and is the author of numerous books for young readers.

For a complete listing of all Yearling titles, write to
Dell Readers Service, P.O. Box 1045,
South Holland, IL 60473.

THE ROOTIN' TOOTIN' BUGLE BOY

Patricia Reilly Giff

Illustrated by Emily Arnold McCully

A YOUNG YEARLING BOOK

Published by
Dell Publishing
a division of
Bantam Doubleday Dell Publishing Group, Inc.
666 Fifth Avenue
New York, New York 10103

ISBN: 0-440-40757-5

Printed in the United States of America

January 1993

10   9   8   7   6   5   4   3   2   1

With love to Jimmy Giff,
a terrific kid

♪ CHAPTER 1 ♪

"**N**ot a sound," Kenny Bender told himself.

He tiptoed out of his bedroom, his bugle under one arm.

He kept yanking up his pajamas.

The legs were long enough to fit a camel.

Outside the hall window, it was almost light.

Kenny stopped to look at the piles of

snow, and the car warming up in the driveway.

His father was leaving for work at Hemming's Bakery.

Kenny could see the red kite too.

It was hanging from the top branch of the birch tree, blowing in the wind.

He tried not to look at it.

It reminded him of his mother. His mother in Riverdale Hospital.

It reminded him of how she got there.

His fault.

His father closed the car door and drove away.

Kenny started down the hall.

He tripped over Eleanor's books.

His bugle clattered down the stairs.

He stood still for a moment, listening.

No one woke up.

If he were a robber, they'd be in big trouble.

He raced down the steps on tiptoe to grab the bugle.

He was upstairs again, at Eleanor's door, in two seconds.

It took him about five minutes to get it open though.

He didn't want to make a sound.

Eleanor was fast asleep, buried under the blankets.

All that showed were her long dark hair and one ear.

She was still wearing a dangling gold earring.

She thought she was a movie star because she had started high school this year.

She was the bossiest thing in the world.

Kenny tiptoed toward the bed . . . but not too close.

He had to be ready to escape.

He was dying to laugh, but that would spoil the whole thing.

He raised his bugle high in the air, just the way Professor Thurman did at band practice.

He took a deep breath.

Then he blasted out the first three notes of reveille.

The professor had taught it to them last night.

Eleanor was out of bed in one move. "Fire," she screamed. "The house is on fire."

She spotted Kenny. "When I get my hands on you . . ." she began yelling.

Kenny twirled his bugle around one finger.

He did an about-face.

He raced out the door and down the hall, holding up his pajamas.

He was laughing so hard, he could hardly get the bathroom door open.

He slammed into it. Then he slid inside, locking the door behind him.

He was safe.

Not so safe.

Six-year-old Justine was pounding on the bathroom door. "Let me in, Kenny. I have to go. Right . . . this . . . minute."

His luck to be born in a house with two sisters.

He opened the top of the hamper. He buried his bugle under the dirty laundry.

Then he sat back to catch his breath.

"You have to let me in, Kenny," Justine kept screeching. "Hurry."

Kenny had to get out of there.

He opened the bathroom window.

The wind blew Eleanor's perfume bottle off the ledge onto the tile floor.

It smashed into a hundred pieces.

Kenny shivered. It was freezing out.

The roof was covered with ice.

Up above, icicles hung from the window like daggers.

He'd probably kill himself out there.

He stepped over the perfume mess.

What a smell!

He climbed up on the sill.

Behind him, Justine was banging on the door so hard, he wondered if she'd break it down.

Eleanor had done that once.

His mother had had a fit.

"What crashed?" Justine yelled. "Kennnnnn-yyyyy?"

He grabbed the window ledge and swung himself out.

Too bad he hadn't rolled up his pajama legs.

He held on to the ledge. At the last moment, he saw the kite. Its tail was whipping in the wind.

Suddenly he remembered. He had promised his mother he wouldn't do stuff like this anymore.

He slid gently down the roof.

He slid fast.

Much faster than he did in the summer-time.

Too fast to grab on to the tree branches.

They were covered with ice anyway.

Brittle.

He fell between them, scratching his arms and his legs.

"Yeow," he screamed.

In a flash he could see the sidewalk, and the evergreen tree.

He landed in his mother's prize azalea bush, the one she said was fifty years old.

Branches snapped all over the place.

He could see the girls coming out the door. And Mrs. Niebling rushing across the street. "I always knew that boy was crazy," she was saying.

He could see his friend Willie Roberts too.

He hoped Willie didn't notice his camel pajamas.

He hoped his underwear didn't show through the rips.

Kenny closed his eyes.

Then he thought about Eleanor and the bugle.

It was the greatest trick he had ever done.

♪ CHAPTER 2 ♪

Kenny held the mouthpiece of his bugle up to his lips. He held his tongue on top of his mouth and said "eeeee" to himself as he blew.

A thin high sound came out.

It sounded great.

"Kenny," Eleanor shouted. "I can't stand that noise."

He got up and slammed the bedroom door.

This time he kept his tongue behind his bottom teeth. "Aaaaahhhhh."

The sound was lower, nice and deep.

He went back and forth. "Aaah . . . eeee . . . aaah."

It would drive Eleanor crazy.

The front doorbell rang.

It rang again.

Kenny snorted. Nobody ever bothered to answer it.

He limped down the stairs, his bugle under his arm.

It was almost time for band practice.

The bell rang again.

"Eleanor," he screamed.

She didn't answer.

She was on the phone again, of course, talking to Harry what's-his-name.

At the same time she'd be looking at herself in the mirror.

She thought she looked like a movie star . . . that blond one with the big teeth.

11

"Justine?" he shouted.

Who knew where that kid was?

Kenny hobbled to the front door.

His knee was still a little sore.

Willie Roberts was kneeling on the steps. He was banging his drumsticks against the doormat.

Chrissie Tripp was there too. "I hear you fell again," she said.

Kenny grabbed his jacket off the living room couch.

He started outside.

"Going to band practice," he yelled back.

Eleanor, that bossy thing, got excited if she didn't know where he was every minute of the day.

He went down the path.

Upstairs Justine was banging on the window.

That pest.

He tried not to pay attention.

Chrissie pointed up at the kite.

It was lying against the top branch as if it were asleep.

"Still there," she said. "How many days?"

Kenny pretended he hadn't heard her.

He stuck the bugle in his mouth and gave a couple of blares.

"How many?" Chrissie asked again.

She wasn't going to give up.

She was almost as bad a pest as Justine.

"Thirty-four," he said.

He could still picture it . . . flying the kite, looping it all over the place until it crashed into the tree. Thirty-four days ago.

He could see himself climbing, see himself up on a top branch.

And then his mother, the world's best climber, coming up to help him, hand over hand, her braid flapping against her back.

He closed his eyes.

It didn't help. He could still see her grinning at him, just before she fell.

"Your mother's been in the hospital thirty-four days?" Chrissie said. "How many more?"

Kenny raised his shoulders in the air. He didn't want to think about it.

Suppose it was fifty days . . . a hundred days?

Justine was banging harder on the window.

"Want to break that?" he yelled.

Justine shoved up the window. "Wait . . . for . . . me," she said. "I'm . . . coming."

Whenever she talked like that, one word at a time, he knew she was going to win.

"Come on, guys," Kenny said.

Before he could get down the street, Justine barreled out the door.

She had one red boot on, and a brown one in her hand.

She was trying to shrug into her coat.

She was a sight.

Her face was smeared with strawberry ice cream. Her fingers were too.

The only clean finger was the one she usually had in her mouth.

Eleanor came to the door. "Take her, Kenny," she said.

Kenny looked at Chrissie and Willie.

"Why not?" Chrissie said.

"She's not in the band," he said.

Justine stuck out her lip.

She was going to start crying any minute.

You'd hear her all the way down the street.

He'd have to take her.

He'd have to face the whole Lincoln Lions Band with a kid who looked like a melted ice cream cone.

♪ CHAPTER 3 ♩

A million kids were running around the gym.

Willie Roberts was chasing Ahmed. He was trying to tap him with a drumstick.

Chrissie was sliding across the shiny wood floor.

T. K. Meaney was sliding after her.

Kenny looked around.

The professor was nowhere in sight.

But Kenny could see Justine.

He had dropped her off at the bleachers.

She was sitting there on the bottom step.

A bunch of other little kids were there too.

They were all dressed up.

He wondered why.

Two of them had fat ribbons in their hair.

They looked ridiculous.

But not as ridiculous as Justine.

At least they were clean.

Justine was a mess.

He wondered if she had combed her hair since their mother had gone to the hospital.

"Look at those kids," Chrissie Tripp said. "I guess they're trying out for twirling."

Kenny didn't answer.

He raced across the gym floor, thinking about Justine.

She couldn't be trying out.

She was clumsy as an elephant.

The professor came to the door. Most of his face was hidden under his fuzzy gray hair and his thick mustache.

Teresa, the drum major, blew her whistle.

Everyone raced for places.

Then they started to march.

Fifes came first.

Then drums.

Bugles were at the back.

That was because the buglers made the most noise.

They weren't supposed to drown out the fifes.

Tonight the band wasn't playing anything.

They were just practicing marching.

They did a lot of that: right flank, left flank, to the rear, march.

They were getting ready for the winter carnival.

Kenny marched past the bleachers.

He took a look at Justine out of the corner of his eye.

She was waving to him, jumping up and down to get his attention.

He frowned at her to stop.

She didn't.

Instead she hopped off the bleachers. She nearly banged into Edwin Wiener on the end of his row.

Edwin had to jump out of her way.

He jumped into John Tobin.

Justine took a little jump too.

She started to laugh.

She thought everything was a big joke.

If the professor turned around . . . if Teresa, the drum major, turned around . . . everyone would think he had a lunatic for a sister.

Teresa blew her whistle again.

Everyone halted.

Everything was still.

Kenny took a quick look to see if Teresa was looking at Justine.

She wasn't though.

The professor marched to the front. "Very nice work," he told them.

He pointed to the kids on the bleachers. "We have some people trying out for twirling tonight," he said.

Kenny gave his bugle a little spin.

He looked at Justine.

She was sitting up straight, smoothing down her hair.

He swallowed.

He hoped Justine didn't think she knew how to twirl.

"Fall out," Teresa shouted.

Everyone rushed for the bleachers.

A moment later, the little kids were out on the floor. Justine was right in front.

Teresa put on some band music.

It blared out of the loudspeaker.

She handed out batons, long skinny sticks.

Justine waved hers at Kenny. She was smiling, excited.

He wondered if she had ever held a baton in her life.

"Ready," Teresa said. "Now."

Everyone began to twirl.

Justine threw hers up, and dropped it.

She scrambled after it.

She banged into some other kid.

The kid began to cry.

Teresa blew her whistle. "Let's start over," she said, frowning a little.

Kenny bit his lip. Next to him, Chrissie was laughing.

The twirlers started again.

Justine was the worst, the slowest. She looked like a baby hippopotamus.

She dropped the baton three times.

The second time she threw it up, it hit her on the head.

At last Teresa shut off the music.

She tapped Justine and someone else on the arm. "Good try," she said. "Come back next year."

Then the professor came out on the floor. "Let's give everyone a hand," he said.

Kenny listened to the sound of clapping all around him.

He tried not to look at Justine.

She was back on the bleachers, down in front of him.

He couldn't see her face. Her head was bent, and he knew she must be crying.

♪ CHAPTER 4 ♪

It was Saturday.

Kenny knew it as soon as he opened his eyes.

It was quieter today. No one was running around, looking for books.

His father had left early.

Saturday was the busiest day at Hemming's Bakery.

They'd bake about a hundred cakes.

Tonight his father would bring home the leftovers.

Kenny could hear Eleanor downstairs.

She was making French toast.

She had burned it again. Smoke was curling out of the kitchen and up the stairs.

Kenny tiptoed over to the window.

Outside, it had started to snow. Fat white flakes blew across the lawn. They covered the bushes in the yard.

The red kite was banging back and forth. Your fault, it seemed to say. Your fault.

His mother had been in the hospital thirty-nine days.

Kenny shook his head. He was going to head up to the college this morning . . . meet Chrissie, and Willie, and T. K. Meaney, the flag holder.

He'd skip burnt French toast for breakfast.

The college kids were working on a giant snowman.

They were getting ready for the winter carnival.

The Lincoln Lions Band was going to march right up there and play a bunch of songs.

Kenny started down the hall.

He went quietly.

He'd slip out the front door before Eleanor heard him. Otherwise she'd be screeching about how much work there was, how he'd have to make his bed, or go to the store.

She thought he was a maid.

He passed Justine's bedroom.

Her school papers were taped every which way to her door.

He stopped to look at them.

There was a page with her name written over and over. Twenty Justine P. Benders.

There was a picture of a red thing on a stick.

A lollipop?

He thought of practice last night.

"I was going to surprise everyone," she had said afterward.

"But didn't you practice?" he had asked.

She looked up at him. "I didn't know you had to. You're always twirling stuff around. It looked so easy. . . ."

Kenny started down the stairs.

In the kitchen right now Justine was crying. "I want my mother."

Kenny swallowed.

He tiptoed through the living room and grabbed his jacket.

"I want my mother now."

"Kenny?" Eleanor called. "Is that you?"

He stopped.

"Your breakfast is getting cold," Eleanor said, coming to the door.

He put his jacket back on the couch, and followed her into the kitchen.

Justine was sitting on the edge of the chair, banging one foot. Her face was swollen and red. The same strawberry smear was on her face.

She hadn't washed.

She looked . . . Kenny stared at her.

She looked as if she didn't have a mother.

If only he hadn't climbed that tree . . . if only his mother hadn't come after him . . .

He went to the refrigerator for milk.

The carton was almost empty.

Wait until Eleanor saw that. She had told him to go to the store yesterday.

She had counted the money into his hand.

"Half a gallon," she had said in a bossy voice. "Count the change."

Eleanor acted like the queen of the world, just because she was the oldest.

He poured the last drop of milk into his cereal bowl and sat down at the table.

Justine was sitting on the other side, still banging her foot against the table leg.

"Why don't you wash?" he asked. He tried to say it nicely, just to remind her.

Justine started to cry again. "I want Mommy."

Kenny stuffed some wheat flakes into his mouth.

He wanted his mother too.

He wondered if she was ever coming home.

Would she make it in time for the winter carnival?

Never.

It would probably be when the snow had melted.

Eleanor slid into her seat. "Eat," she told Kenny. "You too, Justine."

She looked at Justine. "Do you know what a piece of soap looks like?"

Justine put her hand up to her face. "I forgot," she whispered.

Eleanor raised her eyes up to the ceiling. She slapped her forehead.

"Leave her alone," Kenny said.

"All right," said Eleanor. "You take care of her for a change. You're the only one who isn't doing anything around here. Daddy's working a million hours a week . . . I'm—"

Kenny took a bite of toast. "Don't worry," he said. "I will. I'll do a better job than you."

He stood up. "Come on, Justine. Let's go."

Justine stood up too.

"Sure, Kenny. Where?"

He closed his eyes. He could just see everyone up at the college . . . and he was stuck with . . .

"Wash your face," he said. "Wash it right away. Use a ton of soap."

He slammed out of the kitchen.

He was stuck with Justine for the rest of the day.

♪ CHAPTER 5 ♪

It was bitter cold outside.

Kenny swung his arms back and forth.

Too bad he couldn't find his gloves.

"Huppa, two, three-a four," he said under his breath.

He said it the way the professor did, with kind of a roll in his voice. "Huppa, two, three-a four. Huppa . . ."

"The kite is still up there," Justine said.

He didn't answer.

"I said, the red kite—"

"Where are your gloves?"

"I lost them," she said.

He rubbed his nose. He was freezing.

He looked at the jacket Justine was wearing. It had flowers all over it.

She had worn it for Easter last year.

"Where's your winter coat?" he asked.

She raised one shoulder in the air. "I can't find that either."

Kenny sighed. The closets were a mess. So was the laundry room.

He had seen his father down there the other day, shaking his head, trying to sort things out. "If only I had a day," his father was saying. "One day when I didn't have to go to the bakery, or the hospital . . ."

"Don't you have a sweater?" Kenny asked. "Or something?"

"Don't worry." She hopped across a snowpile.

He nodded a little.

They turned the corner and started for the bridge that would take them to the college.

A bulldozer was parked on one side.

His friend Willie's father was making the bridge wider.

Kenny waved to Mr. Roberts.

Willie was standing there too. "Hey, wait up, Kenny," he yelled.

They crossed the bridge together. The noise of the bulldozer was loud in Kenny's ears.

Justine walked along next to them, shivering.

Kenny wondered what Willie thought about her spring coat.

Halfway up the hill were a bunch of kids. Kids from the town. Kids from the college. Kids from the band. T.K. was there, hopping from one foot to the other. And Chrissie, laughing.

Everyone was getting ready for the winter carnival. There'd be ice skating and sledding. Cocoa would be on sale, and marshmallows.

This year, the Lincoln Lions Band would be playing.

They had practiced over and over.

The fifers tooting "Winter Wonderland."

The drummers beating on the drums so loud, you could feel it in your feet.

The buglers blaring away.

And the twirlers . . . a bunch of kids Justine's age twirling those batons as fast as lightning.

Right now everyone was looking at a huge mound of snow and ice. It was shaped into three lumps.

A giant snowman.

In front of it were three boys.

One was standing on another one's shoulders.

A third had scrambled up to sit on top of the other two.

He was reaching out, trying to put a black hat on top of the snowman.

The three of them wobbled back and forth.

"Watch out," Chrissie was yelling. Everyone else was yelling too.

"What are they doing?" Justine asked.

Kenny saw that her nose was running. He leaned forward. "Did you wash your face? That same pink mark is all over your cheeks. What's the matter with you?"

"What are they doing?" Justine asked again.

He sighed. "Wipe your nose."

"What are they—"

"Watch," he said. "Don't you remember last year?"

He pictured his mother, her cheeks red, laughing, pointing.

She had been holding Justine's hand.

"Try to remember," he said. "We were standing right here."

She shook her head.

"Try, Justine. First they put the hat on the snowman, and then the scarf. Mom brought hot chocolate. We had the best time—"

The top boy started to fall.

"Yeow," someone yelled.

The boy landed in a pile of snow.

The other two landed on top of him.

They were laughing so hard, they could hardly get up.

T. K. Meaney was rolling in the snow, laughing too.

"You're too heavy to lift," one of the boys said to the other. He dusted himself off. "We need someone lighter."

"Me," yelled Justine. "I'm lighter. I can do it."

"Shh," Kenny said.

Everyone was looking at her.

His mother always said Justine was so cute.

She should see her now.

Spring clothes. Stains. Hair in knots.

"You're light," one boy yelled.

Justine started jumping up and down. "I'm light," she said. "I really am."

The boy shook his head. "No. You." He pointed at Kenny.

"Me?"

One boy scrambled on top of the other one's shoulders.

"Come on. Shinny up here."

They boosted Kenny up.

It was high.

Everyone was looking up at him.

Justine was looking too. She waved at him.

She was trying to look happy that he was picked.

Her lip was quivering though, and she looked little and cold.

But then someone handed him the black hat for the snowman.

He didn't have time to think about Justine.

He had to get that hat on just right.

♪ CHAPTER 6 ♪

It was almost dark, and snowing a little.

Kenny hunched up his shoulders. He was shivering. Next to him Willie and Chrissie were shivering too.

They had been hiding behind the tree, huddled together, waiting, for a long time.

They had been watching the RIVERDALE HOSPITAL sign. It flashed on and off, on and off, as visitors' cars pulled out of the parking lot.

It was all because of Chrissie Tripp. "I'd die if my mother were in the hospital for forty-two days," she had said.

"Shoo," said Willie. "He can see her sometimes."

"Not alone," Kenny had said. "My father talks about the bakery. Eleanor is always saying how much she's doing, and . . ."

He couldn't remember Justine talking.

It was then, right then, that Chrissie had had the most terrific idea. "How about we break into the hospital?" she had said. "Sneak right in when it's dark, and . . ."

"See your mother," Willie had finished for her.

Right now, Kenny's mouth was dry. Eleanor would be furious. . . . He wondered what the nurses would do if they were caught.

"It's time," Chrissie said.

Kenny looked around. No one was left outside.

The guard had gone into his little house.

Kenny could see him in the window. He was drinking a cup of coffee, looking down.

Kenny looked at Chrissie and Willie.

Then the three of them ran.

They snaked their way around a station wagon. Then they headed for the back door of the hospital.

He couldn't believe it.

His mother was up there in Room 506. She didn't even know he was on his way.

Chrissie was frowning. "How will we get in?" she said.

The door burst open from inside.

A man came out, head down against the wind. "Brrr. Cold."

Kenny nodded a little.

The three of them slid inside just before the door closed again.

They raced across the hall on tiptoe, heading for the stairs.

Chrissie was beginning to giggle, Willie too.

The nurse at the desk never looked up.

They tore up the first three flights without stopping. Kenny's sneakers made a dull pounding sound on the steps. Chrissie was making snorting noises, trying not to laugh.

They opened the door to the fifth floor.

A woman in a blue robe was walking up and down slowly. She smiled at them. "Nice to see rosy cheeks," she said, "and the smell of the outside."

Chrissie was laughing harder.

The woman laughed too.

"Any minute someone's going to hear you," Willie said. "Gonna kick us out of here."

Kenny led the way down the hall. "There," he said. He pointed toward his mother's door.

Chrissie slid into the broom closet with Willie. "We'll wait," she said. "Right here. Don't take too long. Someone will come along and—"

"We just got here," Willie said. "Give him a chance."

Kenny opened the door to his mother's room.

She was sitting up in bed. Both her legs were in casts. They were held up with ropes to keep them steady.

His fault.

Her toes were sticking out of the casts.

She wiggled them at him when she saw him.

"I can't believe it," she said. "It's that rootin' tootin' bugle boy. How did you ever manage . . . ?"

He waved his hand in the air. "Easy."

His mother patted the edge of the bed. Justine's spot. "How's the bugler?"

46

"Fine. I know all of 'Winter Wonderland.' We're going to play at the winter carnival."

He sat on the edge of her bed. "I put the hat on the snowman," he said.

"That's great," his mother said. "Remember last year . . . ?"

"Justine doesn't remember." He shook his head. "She tried out for twirling, but she couldn't really. . . . She was terrible."

His mother closed her eyes for a minute. "If I were home, I would have helped her. I—" She stopped. Kenny could see her swallowing, trying not to cry.

"Next year," he told her. "She'll make it next year."

"That's right." Her eyes were filled with tears, but she was smiling. "Daddy and I were saying that you're such good kids. Everyone trying so hard . . . keeping things going."

Kenny looked down at her feet. It was good his mother didn't know what was going on. Everything at home was in a big mess.

His mother pulled on her long braid. "It's dark out there, really dark. How are you going to get home alone?"

He waved his hand. "Chrissie's in the broom closet. Willie too. We'll walk together."

His mother nodded. "Good." She leaned forward and brushed his hair off his forehead.

Kenny stood up.

His mother reached out and hugged him hard.

Her hair smelled the way it always did . . . like summer.

"I miss you so," she said.

He kissed her on the cheek, a quick kiss.

It would be terrible if she knew he felt a

lump in his throat, that he had tears in his eyes.

"It won't be forever," his mother said.

He nodded once, and ducked out the door.

On the way downstairs, following Chrissie and Willie, he kept thinking about her.

Everything made him sad. His mother was stuck up there in that bed. And the house . . . no one turned on all the lights the way she did. No one made it look right.

And Justine. Somehow, Justine made him saddest of all.

He wished he had brought her with him. Sneaked her in.

He pulled his jacket up around his neck as they pushed at the door.

"Hey, you kids," someone yelled.

They started to run.

They didn't stop until they were out of the parking lot and on the way home.

♪ CHAPTER 7 ♪

It was afternoon, after school.

Usually Kenny raced home.

There were great cartoons at four o'clock.

But not today.

He had thought of the most wonderful plan . . . and all because of Marjorie Allen's little sister.

His mother would love it.

So would his father.

He made a quick stop at the library.

Then he dashed in the kitchen door.

He grabbed Justine away from the sink.

"I'm just trying to get a drink," she said.

"There's no time," he answered.

He clattered down to the basement ahead of her. He held the library book under his arm. "Where's that baton?"

He looked under the old couch. "I know I saw it . . ."

"It's under there," she said. "Some-where."

He reached for it.

"What's that book?" she asked. "Why do you want the baton?"

"Because Marjorie's little sister, Louise, has the chicken pox. Because—"

Justine shook her head. "No."

"Yes." The baton was sticky. He wiped his hands on his jeans. "Listen to me."

Justine shook her head harder. "Lisa. Her name isn't Louise, silly."

"Look, it doesn't make any difference what her name is. She can't twirl with the chicken pox."

"Justine," Eleanor yelled from upstairs. "Did you leave the water running in the sink?"

"I knew it. Something is always getting in the way when I'm trying to—" He broke off. "Don't pay attention."

"I won't," Justine said.

"Do I have to do everything around here?" Eleanor yelled.

"What do you do, anyway?" he yelled.

Justine leaned forward. "Eleanor does stuff," she whispered. "She makes French toast. She—"

"Never mind that now." Kenny frowned. "I'm trying to show you something."

He handed the baton to her, trying not to touch the sticky part.

"Gooey," she said. She gave it a little twirl.

Terrible.

He squinted at her. She wasn't holding it right somehow.

Too bad he hadn't paid more attention to the twirlers.

He flipped through the pages in the twirling book. He stared down at a picture. "Grab it with your fist. Yes. Better."

He nodded at her. "I'm going to teach you how to do this. Then we're going to the professor. Maybe he'll let you twirl."

Justine spun around.

She kept spinning.

"Justine, will you listen . . ."

She stopped. She held her arms out. "Whew, I'm dizzy."

"Now we have to practice. We really have to . . ."

"I'm going to do it," she said. "Don't worry. I've wanted to be a twirler all my life."

She began to spin again.

"Justine," he shouted.

"Oops," she said. "I forgot."

She held out the baton and began to twirl it.

The baton twisted around in her hand.

It jumped away from her as if it were alive.

It hit him in the knee.

"Yeow. Watch what you're doing."

He picked up the baton, trying to get the feel of it, pretending it was a stick from the street.

"Like this," he told her. "Like stirring soup with a big spoon. Just keep going faster."

The basement door banged open.

"There's water all over the floor," Eleanor said.

"Turn off the faucet," Kenny shouted. "Can't you—"

"Of course I did," she said. "What do you think? I have to do everything around here."

Kenny didn't answer.

"Do you have something clean to wear?" he asked Justine.

"No, she doesn't," said Eleanor, leaning over the stair rail.

Kenny closed his eyes. "Can't you find something?" he asked Eleanor in his nicest voice. "She doesn't even have a winter jacket."

"That kid is a walking stain," Eleanor said. "Everything she's got has spots. She should have been a leopard."

"Could you wash—"

The baton flew out of Justine's hand again. It bounced off the wall.

Kenny ducked.

"Sorry," Justine said. She began again.

Eleanor leaned over a little farther. "Hey, look."

Justine was twirling.

"Not bad," Kenny said, nodding. "Now switch hands."

The baton flew.

He ducked.

Eleanor did too.

Kenny checked the book again. "Slip it from one hand to the other. Twist and slip."

Justine switched hands. "I'm doing it," she yelled.

Kenny looked at her.

She still wasn't good.

But she was better.

He looked toward the stairs.

Eleanor was sitting on the steps, watching, smiling.

He made believe he didn't see.

He looked back at Justine. "Twist and slip," he said again. "Twist and slip."

She was almost ready.

♪ CHAPTER 8 ♩

It was time for band practice.

Kenny rubbed his bugle against his sweater. It had a great shine.

Justine was waiting for him at the front door.

Eleanor had combed her hair.

Kenny frowned. "She needs one of those ribbon things."

"A bow?" Eleanor asked. "Wait."

She was back in a minute. She tied a floppy purple ribbon to the back of Justine's hair.

It wasn't great, Kenny thought. It was better than nothing though.

Eleanor handed Justine her winter jacket. "It was under my bed," she said.

Kenny started out the door.

It was snowing a little. He could see the red kite waving gently from the top branch.

He looked away from it quickly.

Justine held up her mittens, smiling. "They were in my jacket all the time," she said.

He looked at her.

She looked warm, clean.

Next to him she began to talk to herself. "Twist and slip, like stirring soup. I'm so scared."

"Don't be scared," he said. "You're as good as Louise."

"Lisa," she said.

Chrissie and Willie were walking ahead of them. They were tossing snowballs back and forth.

"Almost time for the winter carnival," Willie said. He drummed a pair of drumsticks on the telephone pole.

They began to run.

Kenny was out of breath by the time they reached the school.

He waited next to the door with Justine.

"This isn't going to work," Justine said. "I know it."

Kenny thought about his mother. He thought about telling her at the hospital when they all went to visit.

He thought about telling his father.

He knew just how he'd say it, as if there were nothing to it. "Justine's going to be twirling at the winter carnival," he'd say. "Up in front, while I play 'Winter Wonderland.'"

And then Kenny saw the professor. He

was coming down the hall with his coat unbuttoned, his mustache flying.

Kenny went to meet him.

"Louise has the chicken pox," he said. "I mean Lisa."

The professor leaned over. He shook his head. "Too bad. Itchy. Miserable."

Kenny took a breath. "Justine has been practicing."

Justine moved in back of him a little.

"Can you twirl?" the professor asked.

She didn't answer.

"She can twirl," Kenny said. "Really."

The professor smiled. "Want to try it?"

Justine looked up at him. Her face was red. "Yes."

The professor patted her shoulder. "All right. As soon as practice is over."

Kenny opened the gym doors. "Sit on the bleachers," he told Justine. "Don't move."

He looked back at her. "Don't worry."

He took his place

"Mark . . . time," yelled Teresa, the drum major. "March."

Kenny raised his right foot up in the air, then his left.

He could see Justine at the end of the bleachers.

She looked worried.

Really worried.

He was worried too.

The practice seemed to take forever.

At last it was over though.

The professor was waiting at one end of the gym.

Kenny looked at Justine.

She was waiting there, talking to herself.

He knew what she was saying. "Stirring soup, stirring soup."

He went over and tapped her arm. "It's time."

She nodded once. "I . . . know . . . that."

They walked to the professor together.

He looked down at Justine, smoothing his mustache. "Would you like me to put on some music?"

Justine thought for a minute. "I can do it without music," she said. "Watch."

Kenny closed his eyes.

He was afraid to look.

He opened them a moment later when the baton hit him on the ankle.

"Oops," said Justine. She started again.

This time she didn't drop the baton.

She was a little slow, and her feet got in her way.

But the professor was smiling, and nodding.

Kenny smiled too.

He had a lump in his throat though.

He knew Justine had done it.

♪ CHAPTER 9 ♪

It was Saturday again. Winter carnival day.

Kenny fit his bugle to his mouth. He watched until Teresa raised her arm.

T. K. Meaney hoisted up the flag, and the buglers began to play: "Sleigh bells ring . . ."

The fifes chimed in: "Are you listening . . ."

Just ahead, Willie was keeping time on the drums.

If Kenny poked his head out a little, he'd be able to see the line of twirlers over to one side.

He didn't try though.

He kept his eyes straight ahead, just the way he was supposed to.

The professor was counting on everyone to make this a great winter carnival.

Teresa raised her arm again.

They were ready to march.

Still playing "Snow is glistening," the band began to move.

The drummers played louder as they moved forward, up and around the giant snowman.

They passed the twirlers.

Now Kenny sneaked a quick look.

Justine was second from the end.

She stopped twirling as he marched past.

She called something to him.

He couldn't stop to hear what it was.

"What?" he yelled over his shoulder.

Justine leaned forward to yell again.

She dropped the baton, and bent quickly to pick it up.

Never mind, he thought. She was getting better every day.

Even the professor said so.

She looked a lot better too.

They had made sure of that, he and Eleanor, while his father worked overtime in the bakery.

Something popped into Kenny's head. Something his mother had said at the hospital last week.

Everyone was trying now.

It was true.

And something else.

Eleanor had been trying all along. She really had.

Someone poked him with a bugle.

He turned

It was Sean Farmer, yelling something.

Kenny stopped in the middle of "A beautiful sight . . ."

"Your sister, Justine," Sean shouted, trying to be heard over the rest of the buglers. "She's trying to tell you . . . Eleanor said the kite blew down."

"What?" Kenny yelled. Then he realized.

He closed his eyes for a moment, feeling good inside, feeling wonderful.

He began to play again.

The kite was down.

The red kite.

He could hear it in his head, in time with the drums. *Kite is down. Gone forever.*

He played the last few notes . . . "Walking in a winter wonderland."

He passed his father now. And Eleanor. They were nodding.

The band would be finished soon. Then they were going to the hospital.

The nurse had told his father they could bring cocoa and marshmallows.

His father had told them something else. His mother had a surprise for them.

Kenny grinned.

He knew what it was.

His mother had whispered it to him last night over the phone.

She was coming home soon, in one more week.

He couldn't wait.

The best part was, she wouldn't have to look at that red kite.

And neither would he.

He took a breath, and began to play again.